MOTHER HUBBARD'S CHRISTMAS
BY JOHN O'BRIEN

A Picture Yearling Book

To Esther O'Brien,
that mother of mine,
I dedicate this book
—J.O.B.

Published by
Bantam Doubleday Dell Books for Young Readers
a division of
Bantam Doubleday Dell Publishing Group, Inc.
1540 Broadway
New York, New York 10036

Visit us on the Web!
www.bdd.com

Educators and librarians, visit the
BDD Teacher's Resource Center at
www.bdd.com/teachers

ISBN: 0-440-41450-4
Reprinted by arrangement with Boyds Mills Press
Printed in the United States of America
November 1998
10 9 8 7 6 5 4 3 2

OLD MOTHER HUBBARD
went to the cupboard
to fetch her poor dog a bite.

But when she came there,
the cupboard was bare,
so the dog sang "Silent Night."

She went to the woods
to chop him a tree.

But when she got home,
he sawed it in three.

She went to the village
to shop in the stores.

But when she came back,
he locked all the doors.

She went to the driveway
to shovel a path.

But when she came back,
he was taking a bath.

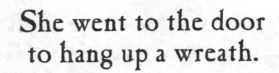

She went to the door
to hang up a wreath.

But when she came back,
he was brushing his teeth.

She climbed up the ladder
to light up the house.

But when she came down,
he was holding a mouse.

She went to the attic
to dig out his skates.

But when she came back,
he was juggling plates.

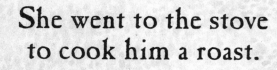

She went to the stove
to cook him a roast.

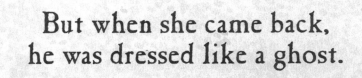

But when she came back,
he was dressed like a ghost.

She went to the piano
to play him a carol.

But when she began,
he hid in a barrel.

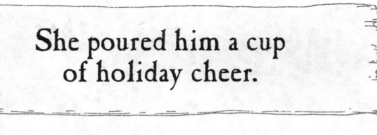

She poured him a cup
of holiday cheer.

She went up the stairs
to get ready for bed.

But on the way down,
came the dog on a sled.

She dreamed in the night
that Saint Nick had appeared.

But when she awoke,
the dog had a beard.

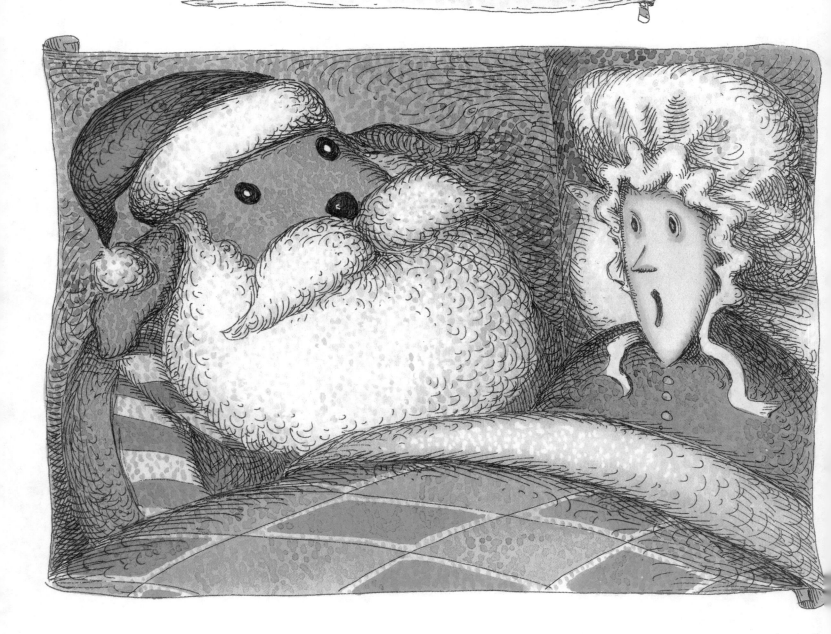

She gave him a gift
and got one of her own.

He got a tie
and she got a bone.

She went to the table,
and there she did sup…

On a holiday feast
the dog had cooked up.

The dame made a curtsy.
The dog made a bow.
The dame said, "Your servant."
And the dog said, "Ho! Ho! Ho!"